D1301995

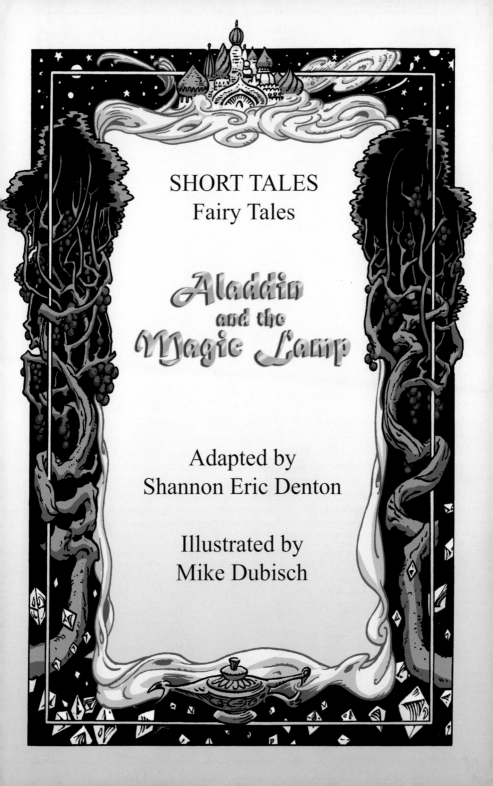

SHORT TALES
Fairy Tales

Aladdin
and the
Magic Lamp

Adapted by
Shannon Eric Denton

Illustrated by
Mike Dubisch

Published by Magic Wagon, a division of the ABDO Publishing Group, 8000 West 78th Street, Edina, Minnesota, 55439. Copyright © 2008 by Abdo Consulting Group, Inc. International copyrights reserved in all countries. All rights reserved. No part of this book may be reproduced in any form without written permission from the publisher. Short Tales ™ is a trademark and logo of Magic Wagon.

Printed in the United States.

Adapted Text by Shannon Eric Denton
Illustrations by Mike Dubisch
Colors by Wes Hartman
Edited by Stephanie Hedlund
Interior Layout by Kristen Fitzner Denton
Book Design and Packaging by Shannon Eric Denton

Library of Congress Cataloging-in-Publication Data
Denton, Shannon Eric.
  Aladdin and the magic lamp / adapted by Shannon Eric Denton ; illustrated by Mike Dubisch.
    p. cm. -- (Short tales. Fairy tales)
  ISBN 978-1-60270-126-7
  [1. Fairy tales. 2. Arabs--Folklore. 3. Folklore--Arab countries.] I. Dubisch, Michael, ill. II. Aladdin. English. III. Title.
PZ8.D436Al 2008
398.22--dc22
  [E]
                              2007036048

In China, a young man named Aladdin played outside.

One day, a magician came to him.

The magician and Aladdin had a fun day in the city.

Then, the magician took Aladdin to see some beautiful gardens.

They walked until they almost reached the mountains.

Then, the magician said some magic words.

The earth shook in front of them.

Soon, a stone with a brass ring appeared.

The magician told Aladdin to go down the stairs and get a lamp.

He gave Aladdin a ring and wished him luck.

Inside the cave, Aladdin saw beautiful trees.

He picked some of their fruit.

Then, Aladdin found the lamp and returned to the entrance.

Aladdin decided he wouldn't give the magician the lamp until he was out of the cave.

This made the magician very angry.

He shouted some magic words and the cave door sealed.

Aladdin was locked inside.

He realized he had been tricked.

He wiped his hand and accidentally rubbed the ring.

When Aladdin rubbed the ring, a genie appeared!

The genie told Aladdin he would make his wishes come true.

Aladdin asked the genie to set him free and the genie did.

Aladdin ran home and told his mother everything.

When he showed her the fruit, he found they were jewels.

Aladdin's mother rubbed the lamp to clean it.

When she did, another genie appeared.

Aladdin asked the genie to get them something to eat.

Poof! Delicious food appeared on silver dishes.

Aladdin's mother enjoyed the meal.

But, she wasn't happy about having a genie in the house.

She asked Aladdin to sell the lamp.

Instead, Aladdin sold the silver so they would have money.

There was more silver with every meal the genie brought them.

Aladdin and his mother did not have to worry about money again.

One day, Aladdin saw a beautiful princess.

He fell in love with her.

He decided he would marry her.

Aladdin needed permission from the Sultan to marry the princess.

Aladdin's mother agreed to help him.

She traveled to the Sultan's palace.

Aladdin's mother gave the jewels from the cave to the Sultan.

The Sultan was very pleased.

But, the Sultan's assistant wanted his son to marry the princess.

The Sultan said, "In three months I will decide who will marry my daughter."

During the second month, Aladdin's mother heard news at the market.

The princess was marrying the assistant's son!

She rushed home and told Aladdin.

Aladdin ran to his magic lamp.

Aladdin asked the genie to make the assistant's son sleep outside in the freezing cold.

The genie made it so.

This went on for many nights.

Finally, the assistant's son ran away.

Aladdin's mother returned to the palace.

The Sultan decided to give Aladdin one more test.

The Sultan said, "Your son must send me forty baskets full of jewels. They must be carried by eighty attendants. Then he may marry my daughter."

Aladdin again used his magic lamp.

The Sultan was surprised.

He said that Aladdin could marry the princess.

Upon hearing the good news, Aladdin asked the genie for a horse and servants.

Aladdin rode toward the palace.

Along the way, his attendants gave out gold.

When the Sultan saw him, he said Aladdin would marry the princess that very day.

Aladdin told the Sultan he wanted to build the princess a palace first.

The Sultan was very happy.

At home Aladdin said to the genie, "Build me a palace of the finest marble."

The genie immediately began his work.

The palace was finished the next day.

The princess set out for Aladdin's palace.

She was very happy when she saw Aladdin.

The two were married that night.

It was the most beautiful wedding the kingdom had ever seen.

Aladdin and the princess lived happily for many years.

One day, the magician heard word of this happy kingdom.

He was angry that Aladdin had the magic lamp.

The magician hurried to the kingdom.

He wanted to steal the lamp.

The magician bought a dozen new lamps.

He tricked the princess into trading the magic lamp.

The magician then used the genie to steal the princess and the palace!

Aladdin promised to save the princess.

He rubbed the magician's magic ring.

The genie took Aladdin to the palace.

Aladdin quickly found the princess and the magician.

He bravely beat the magician with quick thinking.

Aladdin took back his lamp.

Aladdin asked the genie to carry him, the princess, and the palace back to China.

Soon, the princess and Aladdin were home again!

They lived the rest of their lives in peace.